Colour Your Own
MEDIEVAL ALPHABET

PAVILION

First published in the United Kingdom in 2016 by

Pavilion
An imprint of HarperCollinsPublishers
1 London Bridge Street
London SE1 9GF
www.harpercollins.co.uk
HarperCollinsPublishers
1st Floor, Watermarque Building, Ringsend Road
Dublin 4, Ireland

ISBN 978-1-91121-600-1

A CIP catalogue record for this book is available from the British Library.

10 9 8 7 6 5 4 3 2

Reproduction by Mission
Printed and bound in China by RR Donnelley APS

Published in association with the British Library.

Illustrations by Kuo Kang Chen.

The glorious illuminated letters in this book are drawn primarily from the medieval collections in The British Library. The 26 alphabet letters to colour in will introduce you to the magic of medieval book art. Before the age of printing, manuscripts were carefully produced by hand, often by monks in monasteries, and were scarce, treasured possessions. Artists known as illuminators embellished a block of text produced by a scribe with a colourful capital letter, and this collection has brought together some of these beautiful letters from texts that range from religious manuscripts to Latin poetry and specimen letters for artists' use.

The letters are called illuminated, which means filled with light, because they were painted, and often gilded with gold leaf. Use the reproductions of the original illuminated letters on the inside cover to guide your colouring.

The British Library in London was formed from a number of older institutions in 1973. The best-known component of the new national library was the library departments of the British Museum. The Museum's Department of Printed Books was founded in 1753, the same year as the Museum itself.

Over the following centuries, the department grew into one of the largest in the world, sustained by its privilege of legal deposit whereby it was entitled to a copy of most items printed in the United Kingdom – not only books and periodicals, but newspapers, maps and printed music. These legal deposit rights were transferred to The British Library, and 3 million new items are added to the collection every year. The British Library's collection consists of well over 150 million items, including thousands of beautiful medieval manuscripts from which the alphabet collection in this colouring book has been selected.

The first letter of the *Aeneid*, an epic poem about the warrior Aeneas' journey from Troy to Italy and the founding of Rome, a classic of Latin literature written between 29 and 19 BCE by ancient Roman poet Virgil. Taken from a late 15th-century Italian manuscript. (Kings MS 24, f.59)

This illuminated initial from the *Westminster Psalter* depicts David displaying the head of Goliath, David playing a harp, and David about to cut off Goliath's head. Psalters contained The Book of Psalms, a collection of 150 songs originally written in Hebrew, and often also a calendar of Church feast days and some prayers. This psalter was compiled in Latin for Westminster Abbey, England, c.1200–50. (Royal MS 2 A XXII, f.15)

From the *Mirandola Hours*, a 15th-century devotional book produced for Italian nobleman and philosopher Galeotto Pico della Mirandola (d. 1463-1494). A Book of Hours contained psalms, prayers and gospel excerpts, and is the most common surviving type of illuminated medieval manuscript.
(Add MS 50002, f.52v)

The initial 'D[omine]' (Domine is the Latin for Lord) from a psalter produced in Winchester, England, in the late 11th century. Produced in Latin, this psalter had glosses (brief notes of explanation in the margin of a book) in Old English. Psalters contained The Book of Psalms, a collection of 150 songs originally written in Hebrew, and often also a calendar of Church feast days and some prayers.

(Arundel MS 60, f.85)

This initial from a 13th-century Old Testament manuscript shows Jewish warrior Eleazar Avaran in the process of disembowelling an elephant. (MS Royal 3.E.III, f.160v)

From *De Nativitatibus*, the 13th-century Italian astrologer Guido Bonatti's collection of ten astronomical treatises. This manuscript was produced in 1490. (Arundel MS 66, f.170v)

From the *Macclesfield Alphabet Book*, a collection of 14 different decorative alphabetical sets of specimen illuminated letters, produced in England between 1475 and 1525. Such pattern books were used by artists to instruct their assistants or as samples to show to potential customers. This one is named after its previous home, since the British Library acquired it from the library of the Earl of Macclesfield, where it had been kept since about 1750. (Add MS 88887, f.1l)

This interlaced initial 'H[ow]' was used at the beginning of an early 16th-century English grammatical treatise. (Harley MS 1742, f.1)

An initial I depicting the English King Henry VI, found at the beginning of *Nova Statuta*, a manuscript of the legal statutes that had been passed from the reign of Edward III through to that of Henry VI, ending in 1451. Produced in London, 1451–c.1480.
(Yates Thompson MS 48, f.190)

The medieval English language alphabet lacked the letter J, which did not appear until the 15th century. This initial is a 19th-century J from *One Thousand and One Initial Letters*, a lettering sourcebook designed and illuminated by English designer Owen Jones in 1864. Arts and Crafts movement decorative design borrowed and adapted motifs and styling from medieval European, Islamic and Japanese sources.

(1757.b.28)

From "The Hours of Elizabeth the Queen", named after its one-time owner, Elizabeth of York, Queen of England and wife of King Henry VII. A Book of Hours contained psalms, prayers and gospel excerpts, and is the most common surviving type of illuminated medieval manuscript. Produced in London c.1415. (Add MS 50001, f.6v)

Found at the beginning of Matthew's Gospel in the *Préaux Gospels*, produced at the monastery of St Pierre de Préaux in Normandy, France, in the late 11th century. (Add MS 11850, f.18)

This initial is found at the beginning of the Book of Malachi, the last section of the Old Testament, in a Saint Jerome version of the *Great Bible* produced in England in 1405–15. (Royal MS 1 E IX, f.239v)

This initial is taken from the Psalms in the *Arnstein Bible*, a manuscript written by Lunandus, a monk at Arnstein Abbey, Germany, 1172–73. (Harley MS 2799, f.185v)

An illuminated initial taken from the Psalms in the *Arnstein Bible*, a manuscript written by Lunandus, a monk at Arnstein Abbey in Germany, 1172–73. (Harley MS 2799, f.67v)

From a 13th-century religious manuscript, written in Latin. (Arundel MS 156, f.101)

From the *Mirandola Hours*, a 15th-century book of hours produced for Italian nobleman and philosopher Galeotto Pico della Mirandola. A Book of Hours contained psalms, prayers and gospel excerpts, and is the most common surviving type of illuminated medieval manuscript.
(Add MS 50002, f.99)

An illuminated initial S from the *Siegburg Lectionary*, produced at the abbey of St Michael at Siegburg in the diocese of Cologne, Germany, in the 11th–12th century. A lectionary is a collection of scripture readings for worship on a given day or occasion. This lectionary was created in Protogothic script, an early from of Gothic lettering. (Harley MS 2889, f.12)

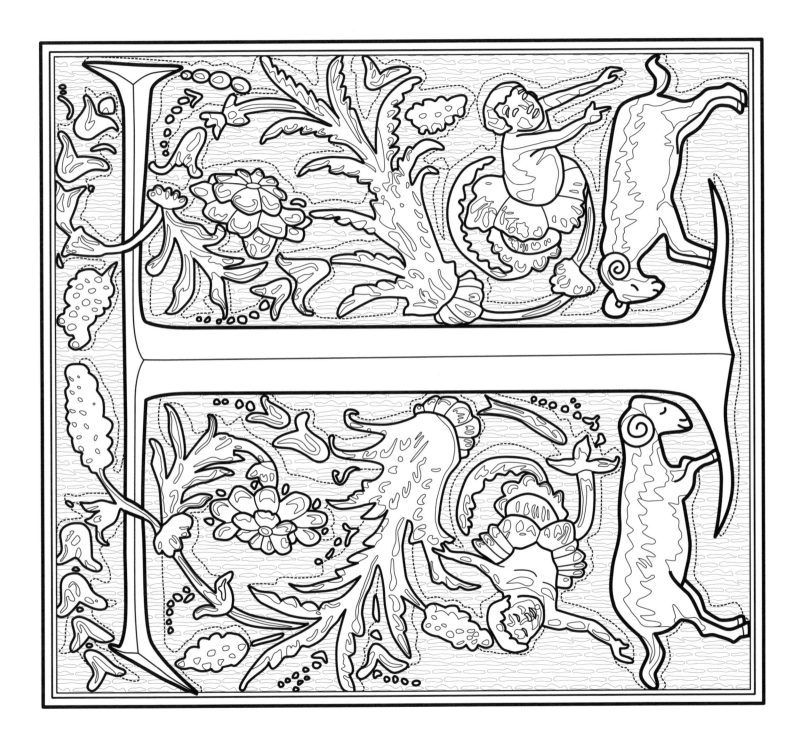

This letter is from the same late 15th-century Italian manuscript of ancient Roman poet Virgil's *Aeneid* as the letter A. The *Aeneid* is an epic poem about the warrior Aeneas' journey from Troy to Italy and the founding of Rome. A classic of Latin literature, it was written between 29 and 19 BCE.
(Kings MS 24, f.37)

From a 12th-century psalter written by, or for, a Benedictine monk. Psalters contained The Book of Psalms, a collection of 150 songs originally written in Hebrew, and often also a calendar of Church feast days and some prayers. This manuscript was written in Lombardic script; today Lombardy is a region of northern Italy. (Add MS 18859, f.39)

An illuminated initial taken from the Psalms in the *Arnstein Bible*, a manuscript written by Lunandus, a monk at Arnstein Abbey in Germany, 1172–73. (Harley MS 2799, f.65)

The first letter of the English poet Geoffrey Chaucer's *Canterbury Tales*, taken from a manuscript dating from c.1410. (Harley MS 7334, f.1)

From the Lindisfarne Gospels, one of the greatest masterpieces of medieval book art. The work was created by Eadfrith, the bishop of Lindisfarne, at the monastery of Lindisfarne on Holy Island off the coast of Northumberland, England, c.700. (Cotton MS Nero D. IV, f.29r)

From the *Macclesfield Alphabet Book*, a collection of 14 different decorative alphabetical sets of specimen illuminated letters, produced in England between 1475 and 1525. Such pattern books were used by artists to instruct their assistants or as samples to show to potential customers. This one is named after its previous home, since the British Library acquired it from the library of the Earl of Macclesfield, where it had been kept since about 1750.
(Add MS 88887, f.24v)

An initial selected from *One Thousand and One Initial Letters*, a lettering sourcebook designed and illuminated by 19th-century English designer Owen Jones in 1864. Arts and Crafts movement decorative design borrowed motifs from medieval European, Islamic and Japanese sources. (1757.b.28)